KEY HUNTERS

THE
MYSTERIOUS
MOONSTONE

KEY HUNTERS

*Getting lost in a good book
has never been this dangerous!*

THE MYSTERIOUS MOONSTONE

THE SPY'S SECRET

KEY HUNTERS

THE MYSTERIOUS MOONSTONE

by Eric Luper

Illustrated by Lisa K. Weber

SCHOLASTIC INC.

For Linda Pratt and her most
excellent okie-dokies

Text copyright © 2016 by Eric Luper.
Illustrations by Lisa K. Weber, copyright © 2016 by Scholastic Inc.
All rights reserved. Published by Scholastic Inc., *Publishers since 1920*.
SCHOLASTIC and associated logos are trademarks and/or registered trademarks of Scholastic Inc.

This book is being published simultaneously in hardcover by Scholastic Press.

The publisher does not have any control over and does not assume any responsibility for author or third-party websites or their content.

No part of this publication may be reproduced, stored in a retrieval system, or transmitted in any form or by any means, electronic, mechanical, photocopying, recording, or otherwise, without written permission of the publisher. For information regarding permission, write to Scholastic Inc., Attention: Permissions Department, 557 Broadway, New York, NY 10012.

This book is a work of fiction. Names, characters, places, and incidents are either the product of the author's imagination or are used fictitiously, and any resemblance to actual persons, living or dead, business establishments, events, or locales is entirely coincidental.

Library of Congress Cataloging-in-Publication Data

Luper, Eric, author.
The mysterious moonstone / by Eric Luper.
pages cm. (Key hunters ; #1)
Summary: Neither Cleo nor Evan like the new school librarian, Ms. Crowley, but they are very curious about where she disappears to at the back of the library, so one day they follow her—and find a secret door, a magical library full of locked books, and a letter from the previous librarian telling them that she is trapped somewhere between the covers of one of the enchanted books and they must travel through the stories in order to save her.
ISBN 978-0-545-82204-6 (pbk.)—1. Books and reading—Juvenile fiction. 2. Libraries—Juvenile fiction. 3. Magic—Juvenile fiction. 4. Locks and keys—Juvenile fiction. 5. Detective and mystery stories. 6. Adventure stories. [1. Mystery and detective stories. 2. Books and reading—Fiction. 3. Libraries—Fiction. 4. Magic—Fiction. 5. Locks and keys—Fiction. 6. Adventure and adventurer—Fiction.] I. Title.
PZ7.L979135My 2016
813.6—dc23
[Fic]
2015023428

10 9 8 7 6 5 4 3 2   16 17 18 19 20
Printed in the U.S.A.   40
First printing 2016
Book design by Mary Claire Cruz

CHAPTER 1

"There she goes again," Cleo whispered.

Evan closed his joke book. "There who goes again?" he asked.

"Ms. Crowley," Cleo said. "Every day, she disappears into the back of the library."

Not one kid in school liked the new librarian. After Ms. Hilliard left mysteriously at the end of last year, Ms. Crowley swooped in to take the job. Although they both had the same brown eyes, Ms. Hilliard's were warm and welcoming while Ms. Crowley's were dark and piercing.

Ms. Hilliard also had a sparkly purple book cart. She taught Evan how to find any fact in a moment and helped Cleo find books she liked. Ms. Crowley only made them sit in their seats and stay quiet.

"She's probably shelving books," Evan said. "Librarians love shelving books. Hey, do you know why an elephant uses his trunk as a bookmark?"

"I don't care," Cleo said, peering down the aisle where Ms. Crowley had vanished.

"So he always *nose* where he stopped reading," Evan said. "Get it? An elephant trunk? *Nose?*"

Cleo ignored him and tightened her ponytail. "I'm going to find out what she's up to."

"Bad idea," Evan said, tucking his joke book into his backpack. "Why do you lose recess every day?"

"Because I don't stay in my seat," Cleo said. "But I had a good reason today."

"I'm sure," Evan said.

"Ellie Fishbein took my pencil. I had to get a new one from the pencil cup."

"You didn't have one in your desk?" Evan asked.

"The pencils in the pencil cup are sharper."

"Uh-huh."

"And they fit better in my hand."

"Uh-huh."

"And they have softer erasers." Cleo looked over her shoulder. "I'm going," she said.

"You're *going* to get punished," Evan said. "A *lifetime* without recess."

"Ms. Crowley will be the one who gets punished," Cleo said. "A teacher should never leave two kids alone. We could get hurt."

With that, Cleo darted between the shelves.

Evan knew following her would only lead to trouble, but he didn't want Cleo to think he was chicken. They twisted through the maze of shelves. Every book he'd ever read smiled out at him like a friend. Here, in the library, he had tons of friends.

"Drat!" a voice said. "Which book is it?"

It came from the next aisle. Ms. Crowley was tugging at books and shoving them back into place. "Literature no longer used," she muttered. "What sort of clue is that? All literature is used!"

"Ms. Crowley," Cleo said. "Is everything okay?"

Ms. Crowley spun to face them. An old-looking brass key hung around her neck. "What do you want?"

"We heard a noise back here," Evan said.

"And I suppose you've come to investigate like two little super-sleuths," Ms. Crowley said.

"We thought you might be in trouble," Cleo said.

"Trouble?" Ms. Crowley stood her full height and towered over the kids. Her black shoes had the pointiest toes and the highest heels Evan had ever seen. "What sort of trouble might one find in a school library?"

"A paper cut?" Evan said.

"Go back to your seats," Ms. Crowley said.

"But we were just—" Cleo began.

"You were *just* going back to your seats," Ms. Crowley said. "Not another word from my junior Frank Hardy and Nancy Drew."

Cleo and Evan headed back to their table.

"Awesome," Cleo whispered. "She called me Nancy Drew."

"So what?" Evan said. "I read one of those books once. Nancy Drew sipped tea and ate something called fancy cakes."

"That's the *old* Nancy Drew," Cleo said. "The new Nancy Drew has a hybrid car and a cell phone. Plus, she solves mysteries!"

Suddenly, Ms. Crowley cried out and the kids heard a sliding sound. Cleo and Evan ran back to look, but Ms. Crowley was gone.

CHAPTER 2

"I told you there's something weird going on," Cleo said. She began tugging at the books. "Help me look."

"Ms. Crowley said, 'Literature no longer used,'" Evan said.

"Every second you waste *thinking about* something is a second you miss *doing* something," Cleo said.

Then Evan remembered.

He charged to the front of the library.

A poster hung on the wall behind the desk. The heading read: "Your Friend Dewey." On the left side stood a cartoon kid with big glasses. Down the right side was a list of different Dewey decimal numbers.

He knew the Dewey decimal system was the way libraries organized their books. Librarians were careful that every book got numbered and shelved properly.

Evan had seen the poster plenty of times before. Near the bottom was a section called *Literature*. Evan read that section closely until he found it:

804—Literature: Code No Longer Used
Literature no longer used.

"Follow me!" Evan said.

He led Cleo to the last aisle of the library.

On the top shelf sat an old, leather-bound book. The number *804* was printed on the book's spine. The title read *Literature: Elements and Genre from Antiquity to Modern-Day.*

"That book looks so boring," Cleo said. "What does 'antiquity' even mean?"

"It means the olden days," he said.

"Modern-day to the guy who wrote that book is probably antiquity to us," Cleo said.

"Just help me," he said.

Cleo laced her fingers and boosted Evan up. Evan grabbed the highest shelf he could. His fingers barely reached the top edge of the book. He curled his fingers around it and pulled.

The heavy book tipped forward. Evan thought it was going to crush them. He leaped

out of the way and they tumbled to the ground.

"What did you do that for?" Cleo said, rubbing her shin through her pink tie-dye soccer sock.

Evan didn't answer. He was too busy staring. Where a wall of dusty shelves used to be, a secret door slid open.

CHAPTER 3

Evan looked down a dimly lit stairway. "We should get the custodian," he said.

"We've wasted enough time," Cleo said. "Ms. Crowley needs our help."

Cleo and Evan stepped onto the first stone stair. Their footsteps echoed. The air felt cold. Suddenly, a sliding noise came from behind them.

"The door!" Evan cried out.

But it was too late. The bookcase slid shut.

"What should we do?" Evan said. He searched for a lever that might reopen the door.

"I guess we take the stairs," Cleo said.

"Are you nuts?" Evan said. "There could be trolls down there. Or evil clowns with vampire fangs."

"Don't be silly," Cleo said, starting down the steps.

As they neared the bottom, a warm light glowed ahead of them. They stepped into the room and Evan sucked in a tiny breath.

The school library forty-two steps above them (Evan had counted) was nothing compared to this one. Bigger than a gymnasium, this library was packed with books of all sizes and colors. Wooden shelves trimmed in brass stretched from floor to ceiling. Balconies, rolling ladders, and spiral staircases allowed readers to reach any book they wanted.

At the back of the library, over a stone fireplace, hung a tapestry that showed an image of an open book. Several people swirled out of the book in a sea of colorful letters.

"The fire's lit," Evan said, grabbing Cleo's wrist. "Ms. Crowley couldn't have built a fire this quickly."

"Maybe someone else is here," Cleo said. "Let's look around."

"Hiding would be smarter," Evan said.

Cleo ignored him.

As they walked, Evan stared at all the books. He saw ghost stories, fantasies, sports stories, tales of adventure, and more. He wanted to open one of the books to see what was inside, but each had a lock on the edge like a fancy diary.

"Look," Cleo said. A brown book with a red ribbon between the pages sat on a table.

The key that had been around Ms. Crowley's neck was sticking out of the open lock. The title was printed across the cover:

THE CASE OF THE MYSTERIOUS MOONSTONE

"What is it?" Evan asked.

"It's a book," Cleo said.

Evan rolled his eyes. "I know that. But of all the books in the library, why is this one out?"

"If Ms. Crowley was around, she'd be able to tell us," Cleo said.

"If Ms. Crowley was around, she'd tell us to go back to our seats," Evan said.

Cleo looked past Evan. "Hey, what's that?"

Against the wall lay a book cart. It was turned on its side. One of the shelves was dented and a leg was bent. The cart was sparkly and purple.

"Ms. Hilliard is here!" Cleo said.

"This cart doesn't mean Ms. Hilliard's here," Evan said.

An envelope was tucked between the bars of the book cart. Cleo took the envelope and opened it. The words were printed in purple ink. Cleo read it aloud.

Librarians speak in hushed voices of a magical library that sweep readers off to different worlds. I never imagined the legends were true—or that one would be right here beneath my school.

If you have found this note, I am trapped somewhere between the covers of these enchanted books.

To find me, travel through these stories and help give each one the ending it deserves. Fail and you will meet the same fate as me.

Succeed and you will discover wonders beyond your dreams. Always look for the key that will move you forward on your journey. I've left clues along the way. Just look for my favorite color!

Signed,

Ms. Sandie Hilliard, librarian

P.S. If this is Evan, go get help. The perils are too great, the challenges are too risky. And you are too fragile.

"I'm not fragile," Evan said.

Cleo held back her laughter. "You kinda are," she said. "But do you think Ms. Hilliard is really trapped inside one of these books?"

Evan righted Ms. Hilliard's book cart. It wobbled on its bent leg. "Maybe *The Case of the Mysterious Moonstone* has some answers."

"I don't see how a book can offer us answers," Cleo said.

"Do you realize what you just said?" Evan asked.

Cleo shrugged. "I look up everything on the Internet."

"Are you ready to open the book?" Evan said.

"What kind of question is that?" Cleo said. "It's just a book."

She reached across the table and opened *The Case of the Mysterious Moonstone*. Letters burst from the pages of the book like a thousand crazy spiders. They tumbled in the air around them and began to spell words. The words became sentences, the sentences paragraphs. Before long, they could barely see, and then everything went black.

CHAPTER 4

Evan and Cleo found themselves in a cluttered office. Gas lamps flickered. A large map of London hung over a desk piled high with papers. In the corner, a small bulldog lay curled on a leather chair.

The dog lifted its head and gave a lazy woof.

"Did we . . . ?" Evan began.

"Did we just get sucked into a book?" Cleo said.

"Awesome," Evan whispered. "Do you think Ms. Hilliard—"

Cleo laughed. "What are you wearing?"

Evan had on a dark jacket with buttons down the front and heavy gray pants. He reached up to feel a round felt hat on his head.

"You look worse," Evan said.

Cleo wore a frilly blue dress, which swayed like a bell every time she moved. She blushed. "Don't you dare tell anyone about this," she hissed.

"Judging from the gas lamps and our clothes, we must be in the nineteenth century," Evan said.

"No way," Cleo said. "My grandma was born in the 1950s, and she had electricity. Lightbulbs, television, and everything."

"No, nineteenth century means the eighteen

hundreds," Evan explained. "You have to subtract a century."

"That makes no sense," Cleo said. She started to go on, but a door opened and a young man rushed in.

"Ah, I see you've met Watson," the man said. He wore a long plaid coat, and his hair was messy. He dumped more papers on the desk. Some fluttered to the floor.

"You must be my new assistants. I had no idea you'd be so"—he looked at them—"so young."

"We're not young," Cleo said.

"And a member of the fairer sex, too!" the man said to Cleo.

Cleo shrugged. "I guess I'm fair. One time, I refereed a soccer game and called a penalty on my best friend."

Evan tugged Cleo's sleeve. "I think he means prettier . . . and more fragile."

"I'm not fragile," Cleo said. "If anyone here is 'fairer,' it's Evan."

"I'm Evan," Evan said. "This is Cleo."

"Pleasure to meet you both," the man said, sorting through a messy pile. "My name is Artie Baker. I'm a detective with the London police. You've been sent to help me solve a crime."

"Are you any good?" Cleo asked.

Artie pulled a treat from his pocket and tossed it to Watson. The dog gobbled it down. "Well, I've had a bit of a bad run," Artie said.

"What does that mean?" Cleo said.

"It means I haven't solved a crime lately," Artie said.

"Lately?" Evan asked.

"To be honest," Artie said, ". . . ever."

Cleo and Evan glanced at each other in concern.

"Well, there was *one* case," Artie said. "My mother misplaced the biscuits she'd purchased at the bakery."

"Let me guess," Cleo said. "You ate them."

Artie grinned. "I see I have two fine assistants."

"You look young to be a detective," Cleo said.

Artie leaned in close. "I lied on my application," he whispered. "I'm only sixteen."

"I don't like the sound of this," Cleo muttered.

"So, where do we start?" Evan asked.

"At the beginning," Artie said. "Detectives must gather clues to uncover the truth. We need to find the Musgrave Moonstone."

"Don't you mean the *mysterious* moonstone?" Cleo asked.

"Whoever called it that?" Artie said.

"That's the title of this book," Cleo said.

"What book?" Artie said.

"She means the Musgrave Moonstone is very mysterious," Evan said.

"What's mysterious, old chap, is that the Musgrave Moonstone has been stolen!" Artie said. "The suspects are at Colonel Musgrave's home. His daughter is to be married tomorrow. The house will soon be filled with people, so we must be swift if we are to solve this mystery."

CHAPTER 5

Evan, Cleo, and Artie heaved open the iron gate and followed the path to the front door. The house loomed above them. Tall windows spanned the gray stone building, and gargoyles stuck out at odd angles. Artie lifted the door knocker and let it fall with a heavy *thunk*.

"Doesn't the moon look strange tonight?" Cleo said. "It's coppery red."

"It's called a blood moon," Artie said. "The morning paper said it only happens once in a long while. This one began at eight o'clock this evening and will end at midnight exactly."

"Blood moon? Midnight?" Cleo said. "That's creepy."

Evan shuddered. "Not as creepy as this house. Even ghosts would be scared of this place."

"I want you to keep all four eyes open and all four ears sharp," Artie said.

Watson woofed.

"Don't forget about Watson," Cleo said. "Dogs are people, too."

"All right," Artie said. "Six eyes and six ears. Keep them all open. A great deal depends on it."

"What do you mean?" Evan asked.

Artie sighed. "The police chief told me that if I don't solve this crime, I'll be sacked."

"Sacked?" Cleo said.

"Fired," Evan said. "It really *has* been a bad run, huh?"

Artie handed Evan a small leather journal. "I'd like you to keep notes," he said. "Write down anything we uncover. No detail is too small."

Artie raised his hand to the knocker again, but the door swung open before he could grab it.

A tall man wearing an orange turban looked down his nose at them. His white jacket was spotless except for tiny splatters of red on both sleeves. "Hmmm—yes, what can I do for you?"

"My name is Detective Artie Baker. This is Cleo and Evan. We are with the City of London police."

"I am Kumar, the Musgraves' butler," the man said. "Please follow me."

The entryway was huge. A giant crystal chandelier hung down, and rows of swords were mounted on the walls. Stone staircases swept up both sides of the room and met on a second-floor landing where a big grandfather clock sat and smaller chandeliers hung.

"The butler did it," Cleo whispered as they walked down a long hallway. "I've seen a lot of detective shows. The butler always does it."

Artie leaned over and shielded his mouth with his hand. "Falsely accusing someone can get you in trouble," he said. "We need to search for two things: motive and opportunity."

"Motive means finding a reason someone would *want* the Musgrave Moonstone," Evan said.

"It's probably worth a bajillion dollars," Cleo said. "That's reason enough."

"Opportunity means we need to find someone who had a *chance* to steal it," Artie said.

Cleo turned to Kumar. "Excuse me, but how long have you worked for Colonel Musgrave?" she asked.

The butler raised an eyebrow. "I used to be first mate on one of Colonel Musgrave's trade ships," Kumar said. "We were hit by a monsoon and lost our cargo, along with most of the crew. I spent three weeks floating on a crate of tea, fighting off sharks with a broken oar. When I finally saw the colonel again, I returned his crate to him. He offered me my job back, but I no longer had any interest in sailing. The good colonel and I have been together many years, and we trust each other.

I have no family, and when he offered me a job in his home, I took it."

Kumar walked on. He led them to a large room. Any part of the wall that wasn't covered with exotic animal heads was covered with oil paintings of old people. A man with the bushiest mustache Evan had ever seen sat at a desk. He wore a military uniform with gold buttons down the front. A woman paced behind him. Her dress was so poofy she could hide a few beach balls under there.

"Colonel and Lady Musgrave," Kumar announced. "Detective Baker and his companions are here."

"Thank you, Kumar," Colonel Musgrave said.

When Kumar had disappeared, Colonel Musgrave stood. He had a wooden leg on his left side. "It's a pleasure to meet you," he said. "This is my wife, Agatha."

Lady Musgrave extended her hand and Artie kissed her glove. Watson sniffed at the hem of her dress.

"The police have already searched the house," Colonel Musgrave said. "The moonstone is long gone."

"Don't give up hope," Cleo said.

"You don't understand," Lady Musgrave said. "The Musgrave Moonstone is cursed!"

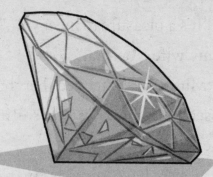

CHAPTER 6

"Cursed?!?" Evan and Cleo said at once.

"Ever since we've had it, the moonstone has brought nothing but trouble!" Lady Musgrave said.

"What sort of trouble?" Artie asked.

The colonel tapped his wooden leg. "In the span of three years, I lost my leg to a Bengal tiger and a dozen ships to pirates. Now, my daughter has fallen ill on the eve of her wedding. I suppose it's best the stone is gone."

Evan scribbled in the journal.

"We're sorry for your losses," Artie said. "Can you tell us about the moonstone?"

Musgrave nodded. "For starters, it's actually a diamond."

"I thought moonstones were opals," Artie said.

Watson woofed in agreement.

"This diamond is called a moonstone because it changes depending on the phase of the moon," Lady Musgrave said.

"How does it do that?" Cleo asked.

"It's a mystery," Colonel Musgrave said. "When the moon is full, the diamond glows a brilliant white. When the moon is dark, it turns gray, almost black. I got it as payment for a large shipment of silk. It's as large as a baby's fist and flawless. Queen Victoria planned to have the stone put on a crown. It would have made her other jewels seem tiny."

"But when the queen saw the diamond change color, she no longer wanted it," Lady Musgrave said. "She believes that jewel is evil."

"Nonsense," Colonel Musgrave muttered, tucking some papers into a folder. The top sheet read "Bank of London" and was stamped "LOAN PAST DUE."

"I'm afraid we'll have to speak with your guests to get to the bottom of this," Artie said.

"Of course," Colonel Musgrave said. "There aren't many people here, though. Most are due to arrive tomorrow."

"Who was in the house when the moonstone disappeared?" Evan asked.

Colonel Musgrave stroked his mustache. "My wife and I were here. And my daughter,

Beatrice, who was the last to see the moonstone."

"Her groom, Richard Cunningham III, was on the third floor," Lady Musgrave said. "He agreed to stay up there. It's bad luck to see the bride before the wedding."

"Wealthy family, indeed," whispered Colonel Musgrave. His eyebrows wiggled up and down like two excited caterpillars.

"What about Kumar?" Cleo asked.

"Kumar is always here," said Colonel Musgrave.

"Was anyone else in the house?" Artie asked.

Colonel Musgrave thought for a moment. "Only Chef Lilith. She's been working in the kitchen."

"How many people know you keep the stone in the house?" Evan asked.

"Great Scott!" Colonel Musgrave said. "We don't keep the moonstone here. We keep it at the Bank of London!"

"We brought it out of the vault just for tomorrow's affair," Lady Musgrave said. "It was to be a surprise at the wedding."

"Unfortunately, we were the ones who were surprised," Colonel Musgrave said. He limped around the desk and leaned against it.

"So, the only people who knew the diamond was here are the people in this very house," Artie said.

Colonel Musgrave thought for a moment. "Just us and our banker, Jules Worthington IV. He dropped it off earlier today."

"Does everyone have a number after their name?" Cleo whispered to Evan.

"Are there any other items of value in the house?" Artie asked.

"Only our grandfather clock," the colonel said.

"It was a gift from the queen herself," Lady Musgrave said. "It's at the top of the stairs on the second floor."

"Splendid," Artie said. "If you don't mind, we'll start by questioning your daughter."

"Oh, can't you let her rest?" said Lady Musgrave. "She's ill and under great stress. Anyhow, Beatrice would never steal."

"That may be true," Artie said, "but we need to be thorough. She was the last one to see the moonstone."

"Very well," Colonel Musgrave said. "She's upstairs in her bedroom."

As Evan, Cleo, and Artie left the room, they bumped into a thin man wearing a silk top hat. He had the shiniest fingernails Evan had ever seen.

"You must be the detectives," the man said, shaking their hands. "I'm Jules Worthington, Colonel Musgrave's banker. The bank is eager to see the stone returned. Now, please excuse me, I must speak with Colonel Musgrave."

"I understand," Artie said. "However, we have some questions first."

Worthington pulled a gold pocket watch from his vest and glanced at it. "I don't have much time," he said, tapping his well-shined shoe on the marble floor.

"It'll only take a moment," Cleo said.

Worthington glanced at his watch again. "Of course," he said. "Anything to help."

"You were in charge of bringing the moon-stone here?" Evan asked.

Worthington nodded. "Our security team delivered the stone in an iron lockbox. We

searched the house, gave the moonstone to Musgrave, and left. Then I returned to the bank. My secretary can tell you I didn't leave until I found out about the theft."

Evan jotted a few notes.

"What's the value of the moonstone?" Cleo asked.

"It's priceless," Worthington said.

"But let's say you were trying to sell it," Cleo said.

Worthington rubbed his chin. "It's insured for more than a million pounds."

Artie gasped.

Evan stopped scribbling in the journal.

Watson drooled.

"That's pretty heavy," Cleo said.

"Pounds are *dollars* in England," Evan said.

"Oh," Cleo said. "Then, that's a lot of money."

"Indeed," Worthington said. He glanced at his watch and then looked out the towering window. The moon still hung red in the sky. "Now, I must speak with Colonel Musgrave. It's urgent."

"Do you mind if we ask why?" Evan said.

"I'm going to insist on removing the grandfather clock from the house and securing it in our vault," Worthington said. "As long as this mystery remains unsolved, we must be careful. The security team will be here before midnight, and I will oversee the job myself. I'm sorry. This can't wait any longer."

Worthington pushed past them and disappeared into Musgrave's study.

CHAPTER 7

When they found her, Beatrice Musgrave was lying across her bed in her nightgown. She coughed into a lacy white handkerchief.

"I was planning to wear the moonstone in my wedding tiara tomorrow," she wailed. "Now the diamond is gone and I've come down with a case of the croup!"

She coughed again. Evan didn't think it sounded very serious.

"When was the last time you saw the moonstone?" Artie asked.

"Nearly two hours ago," she said. "I placed it on my pillow while I fetched some glue." She pointed to a bottle on the night-stand. Goopy golden liquid dripped down the side.

"Why'd you need glue?" Evan asked.

"How else could I attach the diamond to my tiara?" Beatrice said. "When I returned, the moonstone was gone!"

"Was anyone else here?" Cleo asked.

"Only me," Beatrice said.

Kumar entered holding a silver tray. "Your tea, Miss Beatrice."

"Thank you," Beatrice said.

"Kumar," Artie said. "Where were you when the stone disappeared?"

"In the kitchen stirring the soup with Chef Lilith." He held out his arms. "You can see it on my sleeves."

Beatrice poured cream into her tea. "Kumar didn't steal the moonstone," she said. "He's practically family."

"Someone stole it," Artie said. "Someone in this very house."

Beatrice coughed again and then leaned toward them. "I know who did it."

"Who?" Evan and Cleo said at once.

Beatrice held the back of her hand to her forehead. "I can't say!" she cried dramatically.

Watson quietly woofed at her.

"All right, all right! I'll tell you!" She held her handkerchief to her face. "Last week, I overheard a conversation. The person said getting his hands on that gem is the most important thing in his life!"

"Who said that?" demanded Artie. "Who stole the moonstone?"

Beatrice's hands were shaking so much her teacup rattled against her saucer.

"My fiancé stole the Musgrave Moonstone. It was Richard Cunningham III!"

Evan, Cleo, and Artie made their way toward the second-floor landing, where a stairway led to Cunningham's room. Gas lamps lit the hallway, and the deep blood-red moon filled the window at the top of the stairs.

"Oh, the grandfather clock," Cleo said. "Let's have a look."

At least eight feet high, the clock towered above them. The base was made of four carved stags whose antlers supported the case above it. Behind a glass door hung gleaming chimes and a long brass pendulum that swung back and forth. Above that, a silver clock face stared out, as large as a pizza pan and encircled by gems of every color. At the top, a large red ruby glinted at the twelve o'clock mark.

"That's one fancy clock," Evan said.

Artie climbed on a chair and looked closely at the lowermost gem. "Fancy, but fake," he said.

"Fake?" Cleo said.

"We studied gemology in police training," Artie said. "Those stones may look lovely, but they aren't worth much."

They continued across the landing. The entry hall stretched below them. Their footsteps echoed on the floor.

"There sure are a whole lot of suspects," Evan said.

"And a lot of opportunity," Cleo added. "People have been running all over the house to get ready for the wedding."

Evan opened his journal. "There's Kumar, Beatrice, Cunningham, Chef Lilith, Lady Musgrave, and Colonel Musgrave himself."

"You don't think Colonel or Lady Musgrave would steal their own gem, do you?" Cleo said.

"You can never rule someone out until you can rule him or her out for sure," Artie said. "Worthington told us the gem was insured for over a million pounds. That means if we don't find the diamond, Musgrave gets the money."

"Colonel Musgrave has money problems," Evan said. "I saw past-due bills on his desk."

"But what about Cunningham?" Cleo said. "Beatrice said—"

"Let's speak to him before we draw conclusions," Artie said.

"And what about the banker?" Evan offered, adding Worthington to his list. "He knew the stone was here, too."

The chandelier above them jingled. Cleo looked up. Before she could say anything, it began to fall. She shoved Evan and Artie and dove out of the way. The chandelier missed them by inches, smashing on the floor. Shards of crystal flew everywhere.

Artie scrambled to investigate. The chandelier was a twisted wreck.

"That was close!" Evan said. "What are the chances a chandelier would drop right when we're walking under it?"

Artie examined the rope that had fastened it to the ceiling. "The chances were good," he said. "Someone cut this rope."

"Where's Watson?" Cleo asked worriedly.

They heard a woof from the far side of the hallway. Watson was sniffing at the bottom edge of a curtain. Artie pulled it aside to reveal a hook on the wall. A frayed rope hung from it.

"This is where the person cut the rope," Artie said. "They must have escaped out this open window."

They looked out. A narrow ledge wrapped around the building.

"Probably a good thing they're gone," Cleo said. "If they cut the rope, it means they're holding a knife."

She moved close to Evan. "Do you really think solving this crime will help us get out of this crazy book?" she whispered.

"There's only one way to find out," Evan said. "And remember Ms. Hilliard's letter.

Keep your eyes open for a key. And anything that might help us find her."

"One thing's for sure," Cleo said.

"What's that?" Evan said.

"You're doing a great job proving you're not *totally* fragile."

CHAPTER 8

Cleo pushed past Evan and Artie and boosted herself onto the windowsill.

"Where are you going?" Evan said. He glanced nervously at the narrow ledge. "Cunningham is on the third floor."

"The best way to figure out who stole the Musgrave Moonstone is to find out who tried to drop a giant chandelier on our heads," Cleo said. "We need to chase this clue while the trail is still hot."

"Hot," Artie said. "I like that."

Cleo shimmied out onto the ledge. "Let's go."

Artie scooped Watson under one arm. "Shall I go next?"

"I'm going *last*," Evan said.

Artie climbed onto the ledge and edged out.

Evan looked down. It was a long drop to the ground below.

Evan worried about his parents. How would they feel if he just disappeared? He and Cleo had been in *The Case of the Mysterious Moonstone* for a few hours already. Wouldn't someone have noticed they were gone? He must have missed math class and trombone lessons by now. He knew if they didn't solve the crime and find some special key, they'd be trapped in this book forever. But falling from a second-story ledge seemed much, much worse.

Then he thought about Ms. Hilliard. She was trapped in a book, too. He needed to help her. She was the best librarian ever. She was smart and funny, and never pressured Evan to "go outside and get some fresh air." If he didn't help Ms. Hilliard escape, who would? Evan pulled himself onto the windowsill and crawled out into the blood-red night.

Even though the moon looked creepy, Evan was glad it was up there lighting his way. He crawled along the ledge behind Cleo and Artie. His heart thumped in his chest. His fingers curled tight around a gargoyle head.

"One inch at a time," he whispered to himself. "One inch at a time."

"Hey," Cleo called back. "There's a rope ladder over here!"

"Does it go up or down?" Artie asked, shifting Watson to his other arm.

"Both," she said. "It's hanging from a third-floor window and reaches to the ground."

Evan crept over to have a look. Two thick ropes dangled down the length of the house. Wooden rungs stretched between them, spaced around a foot apart.

"We have no way of knowing which way our mystery person went," Artie said.

Watson woofed.

"Not so fast," Evan said. "Look there. Another clue!"

On the end of one of the rungs, a small piece of white fabric flapped in the breeze.

"It must have torn off the mystery person's

clothing when he or she was trying to escape," Evan said.

"Too bad Watson isn't a bloodhound," Cleo said. "He'd sniff that fabric and lead us right to the thief."

Artie smiled. "Watson is full of surprises . . . Watch . . ."

Artie brought the piece of cloth close to Watson's nose. The dog sniffed the fabric and began wagging his tail.

"Which way did the scoundrel go?" Artie said.

Watson looked up and down. A long string of drool dripped out of his mouth and landed on the rung below the ledge.

"Well, that did us no good," Cleo said.

"Oh no?" Artie said. "What's that?" He pointed at the drool on the ladder.

"It's saliva," Evan said. "Spit. Drool. Glistening slobber."

"It's gross," Cleo said.

"Remember the first rule of detective work," Artie said. "Always follow the slobber."

And with that, Artie stuffed Watson into his coat, grabbed the rope ladder, and began climbing down.

Once Artie reached the bottom, Cleo followed. The rope ladder didn't look strong enough to support more than one of them at a time. Evan waited for Cleo to get her feet on the ground and took hold of the ladder himself.

The rope ladder swayed with each step, but Evan thought a ladder—even a wobbly one—seemed safer than a narrow ledge. He swung back and forth. Evan's knuckles scraped across the stone. His fingers stung.

"Hey," Evan called down. "What do you get when you cross a detective with a cashew?"

"Now's not the time for a joke," Cleo said.

"Jokes help me relax," Evan said.

When he reached the ground, Evan looked at his hands. He had scrapes across three fingers on his right hand.

"Oww!" Cleo said, sucking on one of her knuckles. "That stone is rougher than it looks."

Artie held up his hand to reveal a long scrape from his fingers to his wrist. "We match. Now, let's hurry before the trail gets cold."

They followed a stone path around the back of the house.

"So what *do* you get when you cross a detective with a cashew?" Artie asked as they passed through a gate.

"A nut case," Evan said.

"Ha, I get it," Artie said.

Watson lifted his head and began to snuffle.

"Something's cooking," Evan said. "We must be near the kitchen."

They crept to an open window. Just inside, a huge pot of tomato soup bubbled. A wooden spoon the size of a baseball bat stuck out of it. A woman was bent over the countertop with her back to them. She wore a white apron tied around her waist and a tall white hat.

"That must be Chef Lilith," whispered Cleo.

"She's wearing white," Artie said. "And look . . ."

He pointed to her apron. The corner was torn off.

"Just like the strip of cloth we found," Evan said.

Cleo began climbing through the window. "Well, that solves it," she said.

But Evan noticed something else. Her shoes had the pointiest toes and the highest heels he had ever seen. "Wait!" he whispered. He tried to grab Cleo, but she was soccer goalie fast.

Cleo scurried through the open window, marched across the kitchen, and cleared her throat. "You're under arrest, Chef Lilith. Drop your tomato and turn around."

The woman slowly turned. It was their mean librarian, Ms. Crowley.

And she wasn't holding a tomato.

She was holding a knife.

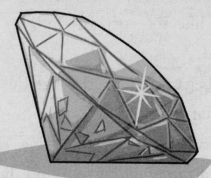

CHAPTER 9

Artie leaped through the window. "London Police!" he cried out. "Drop the knife!"

"Good heavens," Ms. Crowley said. "I was only cutting vegetables." She pointed at the counter where piles of carrots, onions, and potatoes sat. "So much to do for this wedding, you know."

"Ms. Crowley," Cleo said. "It's us. Cleo and Evan."

Evan stumbled through the open window.

"Pleasure to meet you," she said, "but I'm not sure who this Ms. Crowley is. My name is Chef Lilith Merriweather. I studied cooking in Paris and have been working for the finest families in England for many years."

"But you're . . . you're . . ." Evan said.

"I am *Chef Lilith*," the woman said again, "not this Ms. Crowley you are speaking of. I would appreciate it if my junior Frank Hardy and Nancy Drew would stop mistaking me for someone I am clearly not."

She was smiling, but her glare was unmistakable. It was Ms. Crowley for sure.

"My friends must be confused," Artie said. "I've read about you in the *Gazette*. You once prepared a feast for Queen Victoria."

"And a magnificent feast it was," Chef Lilith said. "Roasted quail, cod in oyster sauce, and Cumberland duck."

"Sounds delightful," Artie said.

"Sounds like a stomachache," mumbled Evan.

"If you don't mind, may we ask you a few questions?" Artie said.

Chef Lilith crossed her arms. "You may," she said.

Evan was weirded out. Ms. Crowley was somehow inside this book with them, but she didn't want anyone to know who she was. Why? He guessed he needed to play along to find out. "Where were you when the moonstone disappeared?" he asked.

"I was here in the kitchen with Kumar," she said.

Watson woofed.

"Why did you cut that rope and drop a chandelier on our heads?" Cleo asked.

"What?" Chef Lilith said. "I would never do such a thing, but I did notice a knife missing from my cutting block."

Artie grabbed the huge spoon and stirred the soup. "This smells delightful."

"It's my specialty," Chef Lilith said. "Tomato soup with garlic and basil. Beatrice insisted it be served at the wedding."

"I'm curious," Artie said, lifting the spoon from the pot. "Are fake rubies an ingredient in your recipe?"

He dumped out the spoon. A red stone clattered across the countertop.

"How do you know it's fake?" Cleo asked.

"Fake gemstones float," Artie said. "Real ones sink."

"Someone has tampered with my soup!" Chef Lilith cried out.

"You've torn your apron," Evan said. "Do you mind if we have a look?"

Chef Lilith bunched up her apron and turned away. "I'm very busy."

"It'll only take a moment," Artie said. He took the piece of white cloth they had found on the rope ladder and held it to the torn edge of the apron.

It didn't fit. The bit of cloth was too large.

"Satisfied?" Chef Lilith said. "Now, please excuse me, I've got to fetch eggs for the soufflé. Perhaps Evan and Cleo could help me."

"Of course," Artie said. "I'll just have a look around the kitchen."

Behind the house, Ms. Crowley led the kids down a dark path to the chicken coop. They heard rustling on the roosts. A cluster of chickens slept in the light of the red moon.

Ms. Crowley began rooting around the nesting boxes. She came out with a handful of eggs and placed them into Cleo's gathered dress.

"I'm not sure how you two got here, but you've got to stay in character," she said. "If you raise suspicion that you're not who you say you are, the whole investigation will be over. Artie Baker will be fired and all three of us will be stuck in this book forever." Ms. Crowley began loading Evan's pockets with eggs. "As far as anyone knows, I'm Chef Lilith and you two are assistants to that bumbling detective and his drooling pooch. Understand?"

Evan and Cleo nodded.

"If you got into this world just before us, how did Artie hear of Chef Lilith?" Cleo asked.

"This is fiction," Ms. Crowley said. "We are characters in that fiction, and all characters have backstories. We have to play along."

"This fiction feels pretty real," Cleo said.

"And the stakes are high," Ms. Crowley said.

"You really didn't know about that fake ruby in the soup?" Evan asked.

"No," Ms. Crowley said. "It's probably a clue. Or a red herring."

"Why is there fish in tomato soup?" Cleo asked.

"Not a fish," Ms. Crowley said. "A red herring is a false clue. They show up in mysteries all the time."

"How do you know so much about cooking?" Evan asked. "You're a librarian."

"I watch a lot of cooking shows. Mostly, I'm faking it. I hope you're doing the same."

"What if we enter a book and we're pilots or racecar drivers or astronauts?" Evan asked.

Ms. Crowley filled a basket with the remaining eggs and locked the chicken coop. "Then, you'd better learn quickly," she said. "Now, get back inside and interview your next suspect."

"I think we should go see Richard Cunningham," Evan said.

CHAPTER 10

"Mr. Cunningham," Artie said, pacing across the third-floor bedroom. "Where were you when the moonstone disappeared?"

Richard Cunningham III turned to face them from the armchair near the window. The belt of his velvet robe struggled to stay tied over his round belly.

"I've been in my room the whole time," Cunningham said, pulling his tea tray closer.

"How did you meet Beatrice?" Cleo asked.

"We only met face-to-face two months ago," Cunningham said. "Three years before that, her parents suggested we meet and I sent her a letter from South Africa. I fell in love with her after her first response. Such perfect handwriting! The loops on her Gs are magical. When I finally convinced her to wed, she insisted on this date for the wedding."

"Who else has been up here?" Evan asked.

Cunningham thought a moment. "Other than the team from the bank and the police, only Colonel Musgrave," he said. "He came to discuss our merger."

Watson woofed.

"What merger?" Artie asked.

Cunningham sipped his tea. "My family's shipping company in South Africa will be merging with Colonel Musgrave's in India. Our two companies will be one."

"Who stands to benefit from this merger?" Artie asked.

"Both sides," Cunningham said. "Musgrave's routes in India are risky, too many pirates. Our company needs more influence with the queen. Merging will help us both."

"And how are you at climbing rope ladders?" Artie asked.

"Rope ladders?" Cunningham said. "What sort of question is that?"

Artie reached out the window and began pulling the ladder into the room. "There happens to be one hanging from your window."

"I had no idea!" Cunningham stood and smoothed out his robe. "Anyhow, that ladder would never support my weight."

Evan tugged at the ladder. It felt flimsy.

"What do you know about the Musgrave Moonstone?" Cleo said, narrowing her eyes.

Cunningham smiled. "It's one of the finest stones ever unearthed."

"And stealing the Musgrave Moonstone—" Artie started.

"Stealing the Musgrave Moonstone would do me no good," Cunningham said. "Our companies will be merging. I'll be marrying Musgrave's daughter. The stone was going to be mine anyway. Now if you'll excuse me, I must speak with Musgrave."

Cunningham stuffed his pudgy feet into his slippers and marched out.

"Solving this crime is not gonna be simple," Cleo said.

Artie straightened his tie. "It's a complex mystery," he said. "So, the solution must be complicated."

"We've got too many suspects," Evan said as they went down to the second floor. A railing overlooked the entrance hall.

"And anyone could have snuck away to grab that moonstone," Cleo said.

"Maybe we should go over what we've found," Evan suggested.

They sat at a small table near the giant grandfather clock. The gem-covered clock face sparkled in the eerie moonlight. Artie pulled out some dog treats and placed them beside Watson on a velvet chair. Evan opened his journal to see what he had written . . .

SUSPECTS:

COLONEL MUSGRAVE
- <u>Motive</u>: Money troubles, insurance policy for over 1 million pounds!
- <u>Alibi</u>: With Lady Musgrave

LADY MUSGRAVE
- <u>Motive</u>: Believes the stone is cursed. Wants to get rid of it.
- <u>Alibi</u>: With Colonel Musgrave

BEATRICE

BEATRICE'S TEARS →

- <u>Motive</u>: Last person to see the diamond. Could she have lost it?
- <u>Alibi</u>: She says she was in the hall getting glue

RICHARD CUNNINGHAM III
- <u>Motive</u>: Was heard saying he wants "that gem."

CUNNINGHAM'S SPILLED TEA ←

- <u>Alibi</u>: Alone in his room the whole time

WATSON'S DROOL

KUMAR

- <u>Motive</u>: None. He says he is loyal to the family.
- <u>Alibi</u>: In the kitchen with Chef Lilith

CHEF LILITH

- <u>Motive</u>: Money? Plus, she's creepy and mean.
- <u>Alibi</u>: Cooking all afternoon, Kumar can confirm

TOMATO SOUP

JULES WORTHINGTON IV

- <u>Motive</u>: Maybe money? He knows how much the stone is worth.
- <u>Alibi</u>: At the bank when the moonstone disappeared

"I don't see any clues that tell us who did it," Cleo said.

"We've got to dig deeper," Artie said. "The answer is here somewhere."

Suddenly, Evan heard a clatter above them. A tea cart came hurtling down the staircase, right for them.

"Watch out!" he cried.

Cleo and Artie rolled out of the way. But Watson sat on his cushioned chair munching on his treats. Evan dove in front of the tea cart and scooped him up. Then Evan leaped out of the way right before the heavy metal cart came crashing down. The tray flipped into the air. The teapot and teacups shattered on the floor. When the dust settled, the velvet chair was splintered and there was a huge tea-cart-sized hole in the wall.

"That . . . that could have been us," Cleo said.

"But it was fortuitous!" Artie exclaimed.

Cleo looked at Evan so he could tell her what "fortuitous" meant, but not even Evan knew.

"It means 'filled with fortune or good luck,' " Artie said.

"What's fortuitous about a giant tea cart almost crushing us?" Evan said.

"It means our thief is still in the house." Artie dusted himself off and stood up. "And I know who did it."

CHAPTER 11

Artie paced up and down the hallway. The grandfather clock read 11:54 and everyone was there: Colonel and Lady Musgrave, Kumar, Beatrice, Cunningham, Chef Lilith, and Worthington.

"Oh dear, now the groom has seen the bride," Lady Musgrave said. "More bad luck for the Musgrave family!"

"Mother, the wedding is not until tomorrow." Beatrice sighed.

"I hope this will be quick," Worthington said. He glanced at his watch, which he held in a gloved hand. "My men will be here soon to remove the grandfather clock for safekeeping."

"If we catch the thief, we won't need your men," Evan said.

"*If,*" Cleo said. "I don't see how our clues add up to anything."

"Please, everyone, let Detective Baker speak," Musgrave said. He sat on a leather chair and crossed his good leg over his wooden one.

"At first, I was stumped," Artie said, walking past each suspect as he spoke. "Although you were all in the house, none of you had the opportunity to steal the moonstone. It was with Beatrice the whole time."

"Except when I left the room to get the glue," Beatrice said.

"Precisely," Artie said. "This puzzled me until I realized that trying to discover who came into Beatrice's bedroom might not be the best place to start."

"Get to the point," Musgrave bellowed.

"We know our thief tried to crush us with the chandelier and used the rope ladder hanging from the third floor to move secretly around the house," Artie said. "If we can figure out who used that ladder, we'll know who committed the crime."

"Anyone could have used it," Chef Lilith said.

"Not just anyone," Evan said. "Colonel Musgrave has a wooden leg. He could never step on the rungs."

"And Lady Musgrave's poofy skirts would have gotten in the way," Cleo said.

Artie looked Cunningham up and down. "Cunningham, you're way too heavy to have used the ladder," he said.

"I'm not *that* heavy," Cunningham said, sucking in his belly. "But in this case, I'm glad to be carrying a few extra pounds."

"And by that you don't mean British money, right?" Cleo said. She bent down and scratched Watson behind the ears.

"We saw Beatrice and Kumar in Beatrice's room just before the chandelier fell on us, so we know neither of them could have cut the rope," Evan said.

Artie strode across the carpeted hallway and stood in front of Worthington. "That leaves just one person," Artie said.

Worthington took a tiny step back. "What are you suggesting?" he asked.

"I'm not *suggesting* anything," Artie said. I'm *saying* that Jules Worthington IV stole the Musgrave Moonstone!"

"Preposterous!" Worthington said. "I have witnesses to prove I was at the bank when the moonstone disappeared."

Artie sighed. "And that's where I'm stumped," he said.

"You can't go around accusing people of crimes," Worthington said. "Now, if you'll excuse me, I need to meet my men downstairs so they can move the clock."

Evan felt the sting from the scrape on his right hand, and that gave him an idea. "What if I can prove you were on that rope ladder?" he said.

"You couldn't possibly . . ." Worthington said.

"Why are you wearing gloves?" Evan asked.

"It's a bit chilly tonight," Worthington said shiftily.

"No, it's not," Kumar said, stepping around the smashed chandelier. "It's warmer than Rajasthan in late August."

"I noticed Worthington's shiny fingernails when we first met him," Evan said. "Now he's wearing gloves. We scraped our hands climbing down the rope ladder. I'll bet Worthington did, too."

"Worthington was with the bank team when they searched the house," Cleo said. "He could have attached the rope ladder to the windowsill then."

"Worthington, remove your gloves," Colonel Musgrave said.

Worthington glared at Musgrave and then peeled off his gloves. A large scrape stretched from his wrist to his knuckles. "This doesn't prove anything," he said. "I could have gotten this scrape anywhere. Without the diamond, without proving how it was stolen, you have no case. Now, I must insist—"

"I must insist you stay right where you are," Evan said. He walked across the hallway and stood in front of the huge grandfather clock. "I know where the Musgrave Moonstone has been hiding all along!"

CHAPTER 12

Evan climbed on a chair and swung open the glass covering the clock face. It was almost midnight, and the colored gems marking each hour sparkled in the moonlight.

"None of those are the Musgrave Moonstone," Lady Musgrave said. "Those gems are all colored: red, yellow, blue, green, and purple!"

"Colonel Musgrave said the moonstone changes depending on the phase of the moon,"

Evan said. "It glows bright white when the moon is full and turns gray, almost black, when there's no moon."

"What does that prove?" Cunningham asked.

"Tonight is the blood moon," Evan said. "If the stories about the diamond are true, it should have turned red tonight, at least until the blood moon ends."

Artie looked at the clock. "And that should be right about now," he said.

The chimes inside the grandfather clock began to toll. Twelve bells for midnight.

Through the window, the deep red of the blood moon faded to a pale orange and, soon after, to white.

The bright red stone that sat over the twelve on the clock face changed, too, from a deep red, to pale orange, to brilliant white.

"The moonstone!" Colonel Musgrave cried out.

"I have the gem from the clock right here," Artie said, pulling it from his pocket. "It was floating in Chef Lilith's soup."

"Then Chef Lilith stole the moonstone!" Worthington said. "I was at the bank! I have witnesses!"

"That's what's tough about this crime," Cleo said. "It's a complex mystery."

Artie perked up. "So, the solution must be complicated!" he said. "Of course! There were *two* people involved!"

Everyone began looking at one another.

"Well, who was it?" Lady Musgrave said, placing a hand on her husband's shoulder.

Cleo winked at Evan. "You may not be as fragile as you seem," she whispered, "but I'm also not as dim."

"I never said you were dim," Evan said.

"Out with it," Colonel Musgrave said. "Who did it?"

Cleo looked down the line of suspects. "The person who helped steal the Musgrave Moonstone was Beatrice Musgrave!"

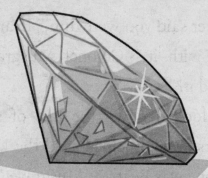

CHAPTER 13

"I—I did no such thing!" Beatrice shrieked. She placed the back of her hand on her forehead, lay down across a long sofa, and fanned herself with her handkerchief.

"There," Cleo said, pointing at the clock. "It's the same glue you had in your bedroom. I can see it around the edge of the diamond." She grabbed a spoon from the broken tea set, climbed up next to Evan, and carefully pried the gemstone from the face of the clock. "You left your room at eight, replaced the stone on the clock with the Musgrave Moonstone, and used the ladder to climb down to the kitchen. Your handkerchief protected your hand from getting scraped. Once there, you dropped the stone from the clock into the soup."

"You insisted on Chef Lilith's famous tomato soup for your wedding," Evan said. "That's because it's hard to see a red stone in red soup!"

"Tomato, garlic, and basil soup," Chef Lilith corrected him, holding up her giant spoon. "It's famous."

"Your plan might have worked if you knew more about fake gems," Artie said. "Fake gems float."

"It was Richard!" Beatrice said. "I heard him say that acquiring the gem is the most important thing in his life!"

"I was speaking to your father about you, my little emerald!" Cunningham said.

"This is too much for me to handle!" Beatrice cried. "I'm too fragile!"

Cleo and Evan hopped down.

Colonel Musgrave crossed the hallway and took his daughter's hand. "Dearest Beatrice," he said. "Is it true? Did you plan this theft?"

Cunningham dropped to his knee beside Beatrice. "Were you never planning to marry me, my fluffy monkey?" he asked.

"You look nothing like the photograph you sent," Beatrice said. "Anyhow, we both know this marriage is more about my father's company than about me. Plus, the mosquitoes in South Africa are larger than house cats!" Beatrice began to weep into her handkerchief.

Evan noticed a piece of it was torn off.

"Look," Evan said. He held up the scrap of fabric they had found on the rope ladder. "It's a perfect fit."

"It was Worthington's idea!" Beatrice cried. "He said no one would be hurt. He said the insurance company would pay Daddy for the lost diamond and we would sell the moonstone and be happy together!"

"This is absurd," Worthington said, sneering. "The worst detective on the London police force and two brats figuring out my plans? I was supposed to be on my way to America by now!"

"America?" Beatrice wailed. "You told me to meet you on the ship to *Italy*!"

Worthington's face twitched. "Plans change, bunny." He lunged across the hallway and snatched the Musgrave Moonstone from Cleo. Worthington turned to run, but Watson snapped his teeth onto the banker's pants and snarled. Evan and Cleo grabbed hold of his arms. But Worthington pulled free of them all.

Whack!

That's when Chef Lilith conked him on the head with her giant spoon.

Worthington dropped to the floor, dazed. One boat ticket to America fell from his pocket.

Kumar clutched Worthington's jacket. "The only trip you'll be taking is to jail," he said.

"I've always wanted to say that," Artie said, disappointed.

"Feel free," Kumar said.

Artie turned to Worthington and opened his mouth to speak. He exhaled. "Well, now you've taken all the fun out of it," he said.

"Why don't you find the fun in putting on the handcuffs?" Evan said.

"Grand idea!" Artie said. He pulled out a set of iron handcuffs and snapped them on Worthington's wrists. "The only banking you'll be doing . . ." Artie paused. "Is banking . . . in jail."

"That made no sense," Evan said.

"Yes, I'll have to work on that," Artie said. "In the meantime, I'll send word to Chief Rutherford that this crime has been solved."

Watson woofed.

Cleo clapped. "Your job is saved!" she said.

"It looks that way." Artie began emptying his pockets. He pulled out a sealed purple envelope and handed it to Cleo. "Give me a moment while I find the key to the handcuffs."

The key. Evan and Cleo glanced at each other.

After loading most of a table with loose change, scraps of paper, and dog treats, Artie finally pulled out a thin chain. A silver key with swirling designs dangled from it. He held it out to the kids.

"Hold this for me," Artie said. "I don't want to lose it."

"Do you mind if I hold it as well?" Chef Lilith said. "I've always been interested in police work."

"Certainly," Artie said.

Evan, Cleo, and Chef Lilith grabbed the chain. Letters burst from the key like a thousand crazy spiders. The letters tumbled in the air around them and began to spell words. The words became sentences, the sentences paragraphs. Before long, they could barely see. And then everything went black.

CHAPTER 14

"Wake up," Ms. Crowley snapped.

Evan opened his eyes and lifted his head from the table. Cleo was sitting across from him. She must have dozed off, too. Plain wooden shelves surrounded them. The poster explaining the Dewey decimal system hung on the wall behind the checkout desk. They were back in their school library. Evan glanced at the clock. Only five minutes had passed.

Ms. Crowley loomed over them. "You're here to do your work, not to nap," she barked. "Now, gather your things. Recess is over."

Evan wiped a string of drool from his cheek.

"You're . . . you're not wearing that crazy suit," Cleo said to him.

"You remember that?" Evan said.

Cleo leaned across the table to whisper, "Two people can't be in the same dream, can they?"

"I don't think so," Evan said.

The bell rang.

"Go." Ms. Crowley began to tap her foot. "I have a kindergarten read-aloud in five minutes."

Evan slung his backpack onto his shoulders. "Ms. Crowley, do you like watching cooking shows on television?"

"Stop talking nonsense," Ms. Crowley said. "And stop burying your nose in all those books. They'll rot your brain."

But as they passed her into the hallway, Evan could swear he smelled tomato soup.

Kids began to fill the hallways as they came in from the playground.

"What do we do now?" Cleo asked. "Do we go on as though we didn't just solve a major crime?"

"I'm not sure," Evan said.

He felt a lump in his pocket. He reached in and pulled out a thin chain. A small silver key hung from it.

Evan's eyes brightened and he showed the key to Cleo.

Cleo patted her pockets and pulled out a purple envelope. She tore it open.

Evan, if you're reading this letter, I'm proud of you. In my last note, I warned you that you were too fragile, but only someone who loves stories as you do would have found the Lost Library.

I know telling you to go no further would be a waste of time, but please use caution. I hope you've brought a friend along. The Case of the Mysterious Moonstone is nothing compared to the challenges to come.

I'm not sure which librarian took my place at school, but not all of them are kind. Some may try to use the Lost Library for evil. Be wary.

Your friend
and librarian,
Ms. Sandie Hilliard

"If it didn't happen to me, I'd never believe it," Evan said.

"It did happen to us, and I still don't believe it!" Cleo said.

They walked down the hallway toward their next class. "I do know one thing," Evan said.

"What?" Cleo asked.

"I'm going back to the library tomorrow," he said. "We need to find Ms. Hilliard and stop Ms. Crowley from whatever she's up to."

Cleo grinned. "See you there, Sherlock!"

The Lost Library is full of exciting—and dangerous—books! And Evan and Cleo have a magical key to open one of them. Where will they end up next? Read on for a sneak peek of *The Spy's Secret*!

"Ugh, why does Mrs. Cabanos give us boring crossword puzzles for homework?" Cleo asked Evan across the library table. "What's a four-letter word for 'fake butter'?"

Evan didn't look up from his math. "Oleo," he said.

"What about a three-letter word for 'anger'?"

"Ire."

" 'Sea eagle'?"

"Erne."

"Jai—"

"Alai."

Cleo's pencil fell from her fingers. "How do you know all this stuff?"

Evan shrugged. "My parents do the cross-word every weekend."

"I read the comics every weekend," Cleo said. "How come we don't get homework about that?"

"Don't you get a great feeling when you finish a puzzle?" Evan asked. "Like you can accomplish anything?"

Cleo shook her head. "Puzzles give me headaches. Anyhow, no one says that."

"Says what?"

Cleo made a serious face and sat tall in her seat. " 'Honey, would you please pass the *oleo*? I'd like to spread it on my toast.' "

Evan laughed. "I don't think it's a word people use anymore."

"Then what's the point of giving us homework about it?"

"I have no idea," Evan said.

"I . . . have . . . no . . . idea . . . !" a voice said mockingly. It was Ms. Crowley, their not-so-nice librarian. She walked up behind Evan.

A few days earlier, Ms. Crowley had led them to the magical library hidden under their school. It was she who showed them that any book they opened would sweep them off to the world inside that book. It was because of her that Evan and Cleo felt they might find their first librarian, Ms. Hilliard, who had mysteriously disappeared into one of those books.

Each word Ms. Crowley said was punctuated by the sharp click of her pointy, uncomfortable-looking high heels. "What do you 'have no idea' about?"

"I just said 'oleo' isn't a word people use anymore," Evan said. "People say 'margarine.'"

"Or they don't say it at all," Cleo said. "Margarine is bad for you."

Ms. Crowley circled their table like a hungry wolf. "Maybe *I* use the word 'oleo,'" she said. "Why don't you ask me?"

"Umm . . . okay," Evan said. "Ms. Crowley, do you ever say 'oleo'?"

"This is a quiet study period!" she barked. "Two days of detention for both of you!"

"But . . ." Cleo said.

"Quiet!" Ms. Crowley barked again. "Now it's four days!"

Evan raised his hand.

"Yes?" Ms. Crowley said.

"I was just wondering . . ."

"I told you to be quiet," Ms. Crowley said. "That's eight days!"

"But I—"

"Sixteen days!" She bent down so her face was close to Evan's. "Do you want to try for thirty-two?"

Evan began to open his mouth, but closed it again.

"That's better," Ms. Crowley said. "Now, there may be something you could do to get me to forget about all this detention. One of you holds a key that unlocks a certain book. If you gave me that key, I might forget about your sixty-four days of detention."

"Sixty-four?" Cleo burst out. "It was sixteen!"

"Now it's one hundred and twenty-eight!" Ms. Crowley bellowed. "Won't Principal Flynn be disappointed in her star pupil and her star athlete? Won't your parents be upset?"

"I . . . I . . ." Evan's hand moved to his pocket. He felt the lump made by the key they had gotten at the end of their last adventure.

Cleo stood. "I left it at home."

Ms. Crowley smiled a toothy grin. "Be sure to bring it tomorrow," she said. "A strange underground library is no place for children."

Ms. Crowley clicked back to the front desk and began stamping books loudly.

Evan wiggled his fingers into his pocket. The key was warm from pressing against his leg all day. He pulled it out by its chain and held it up. As it spun, the key glinted in the light from the window.

Cleo snatched it and darted between the bookshelves.

"Wait!" Evan hissed.

"Wait!" Ms. Crowley called after them.

Evan chased Cleo through the maze of shelves until they reached the nonfiction section. Cleo scampered up the bookcase, stretched as high as she could, and grabbed hold of the huge, dusty, boring-looking book titled *Literature: Elements and Genre from Antiquity to Modern-Day*.

The book tipped forward. The secret bookcase swung open.

Evan followed Cleo down the stairs and

into the magical room beneath their elementary school. Even though he'd seen it before, the library still amazed him. The shelves, sliding ladders, and spiral staircases were made of dark wood and stretched into darkness above them. Catwalks and balconies reached around corners and across gaps to let readers explore every nook. At the back of the library, over a stone fireplace, hung a tapestry that showed an image of an open book with people swirling into it among a sea of colorful letters.

The fire in the fireplace burst to life, sending out a warm glow.

"We have to hurry," Cleo said. "Ms. Crowley is right behind us."

"There are thousands of books in this library," Evan said. "How do we know which one to choose?"

"Any of them," Cleo said. She grabbed a book off the shelf. The title read *The Jumpy Puppy*. The cover had a picture of a brown puppy sitting in its water bowl. "Let's go here. There's nothing scary or dangerous about jumpy puppies."

"Jumpy puppies aren't potty trained," Evan said.

"That's nothing compared to a chandelier almost falling on our heads like in *The Case of the Mysterious Moonstone*."

"Good point," Evan said.

Cleo jiggled the key against the tiny key-hole. "It doesn't fit."

Evan heard a metallic clank. A rolling ladder with brass rungs slid along a track and stopped in front of them.

"I guess we go up," Evan said.

Cleo grabbed the first rung and started to climb. Evan followed. When they reached the top of the ladder, sharp heels sounded on the stone floor below.

"Come down this instant!" Ms. Crowley hollered.

"Hurry!" Cleo ran along a metal catwalk, which wrapped around several walls of bookshelves.

Evan followed her. "Where are we going?" he asked.

"Away from Ms. Crowley!"

They reached the end of the catwalk. Evan felt dizzy. The ground was thirty feet below them, and he hated heights. Cleo grabbed a rope that was tied to the railing. It stretched into the darkness above them. She stuffed it into Evan's hands.

"Hold on tight!" she said.

"What are you do—"

But before Evan could finish his sentence, Cleo had flung them out into open space. Air whooshed past Evan's ears. His stomach flip-flopped. They swung across the library and landed on another balcony.

"There!" Cleo pointed to a small desk. A lamp shone on a blue book with a silver lock on the cover. The title read *The Viper's Secret*.

"That's it," she said.

Evan's heart was still pounding in his chest. "How do you know?"

"The key matches the lock."

"Lots of things are silver," Evan said.

Cleo ignored him and slid the key into the lock. It fit perfectly.

"Stop!" Ms. Crowley screamed. They looked up to see her on the edge of the catwalk behind them. The rope was swinging back and forth. Ms. Crowley reached for it each time it came close. "Don't turn that key!"

Cleo grinned. "I'd never disobey my school librarian," she said.

She held the key tight and spun *The Viper's Secret* on the desk. The lock popped open. Letters burst from the pages of the book like a thousand crazy spiders. They tumbled in the air around them and began to spell words. The words turned into sentences, the sentences paragraphs. Before long, they could barely see through the letter confetti.

Then everything went black.

JOIN THE RACE!

It's an incredible adventure through the animal kingdom, as kids zip-line, kayak, and scuba dive their way to the finish line! Packed with cool facts about amazing creatures, dangerous habitats, and more!

scholastic.com